Littlest Pet Shop

RAPUNZEL

by Samantha Brooke
illustrated by Jim Talbot

SCHOLASTIC INC.

New York   Toronto   London   Auckland   Sydney
Mexico City   New Delhi   Hong Kong   Buenos Aires

ISBN-13: 978-0-545-00795-5
ISBN-10: 0-545-00795-X

12 11 10 9 8 7 6 5   9 10 11 12/0

Printed in the U.S.A.
First printing, March 2008

Once upon a time there was a puppy named Rapunzel.

Rapunzel lived next to a pretty garden.
The garden belonged to the queen.

The queen never let anyone inside her garden. The fruit in the queen's garden looked very good.

One day, Rapunzel snuck into the garden.

She wanted to try some of the queen's fruit.

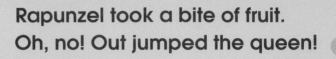

Rapunzel took a bite of fruit.
Oh, no! Out jumped the queen!

6

The queen was angry.
She put a leash on Rapunzel and locked her in a tall tower.

Each time the queen came, she said,
"Rapunzel, Rapunzel, let down your leash."

When Rapunzel let down her leash,
the queen climbed up the tower.

The queen came every day.

But she would not set Rapunzel free.

When Rapunzel was alone, she listened to the birds sing.
Sometimes Rapunzel barked along.

One day, a prince was swinging by. He heard a sweet song. He wanted to meet the pet with the pretty voice.

The prince was good at climbing,
but the tower walls were slippery.
He could not get in. So the prince
hid and waited.

Later, the queen came to the tower.
The prince heard her say, "Rapunzel,
Rapunzel, let down your leash."

The prince saw the queen
climb up the tower.

After the queen left, the prince
said, "Rapunzel, Rapunzel, let down
your leash."

Rapunzel let down her leash.
The prince climbed up the tower.

The prince wanted to set Rapunzel free,
but he did not know how.

The prince promised to come back to
help Rapunzel.

The next day, the prince came.

He had an idea.

The birds could help him free Rapunzel!

They could carry Rapunzel and the prince to the ground.

Then the queen came to the tower.

26

She did not see Rapunzel and the prince in the sky.

"Rapunzel, Rapunzel, let down your leash,"
the queen said.

28

And that's just what Rapunzel did!

From that day on, Rapunzel and the prince
lived happily ever after.